To the Pool with Mama

by Sue Farrell
art by Robin Baird Lewis

Annick Press Ltd.
Toronto • New York • Vancouver

Today is Friday. It is the day that I go to the pool.

"Pool, pool, pool!" I say.

I pull my towel out of the cupboard and get my swimsuit from the dresser. Mama helps me put them in my backpack.

Mama walks with me to the place that has the pool. When we get to the change room, she wants me to take off my clothes and put on my swimsuit. I want to close all the little closets.

I go inside of one. I fit just right.
"Mama! Mama!" I say.
Mama opens the closet where I
am hiding. I say, "Boo!"
"Eeeek!" Mama says.
She helps me jump out.
"Come on," she says. "You have
to get into your swimsuit now."

I take wee baby steps on the way to the pool. The floor is smooth and slippery and wet on my bare naked feet. Then the floor gets prickly, pokey and pebbly.

"Ow! Ow! Ow!" I say.

A girl is in the shower. Water shoots on her head and runs down her swimsuit. It makes a mess on the floor. She rubs shampoo in her hair.

The water and the shampoo make a white river that slides down to her feet. The river goes to a small circle on the floor. It doesn't come back.

Mama lifts me up so I can push
the button. More water comes out of the wall. It feels
like a hundred raindrops on my skin. It gets me wet.

I run out of the cool water and grab Mama's hand. "Let's
go," she says.

I push and push and push on the heavy door.
It doesn't open. Mama helps me.

"Let me carry your towel," Mama says. "It's slippery here and we have to hold hands."

"No!" I say. I hold my towel with one hand and I hold Mama with one hand. We walk to the baby pool.

The pool is noisy and it smells like cleaning. It is like a big bathtub for lots of kids.

The baby pool has water that squirts from the wall. There are balls, and buckets, and toy ducks—even a watering can.

I jump with two feet into the pool. The water tickles my ankles. I lay down so my belly touches the bottom of the pool. I splash water everywhere with my arms and legs. I like making a mess.

I fill up the bucket to bring
to Mama. It is heavy. The water
is jiggly.

I drop the bucket. Water falls
all over Mama's legs and all
over Mama's toes.

"John J.!" she says. "You must
keep the water in the pool."

I see a circle on the
floor. It is like the one in
the shower room.

I dump my bucket of
water on top of the circle. The
water goes away. I look and look,
but I can't find my water. I put my
eyes really close to the round part,
but I still can't find my water.

"Look," Mama says. "There's Elise."

Elise has a bucket of water too.
She dumps her water on my head.
  "Mama, Mama!" I cry.

Mama wipes the water from my face.

"It's OK," she says. Mama hugs me. "I think it's time to go."

Mama wraps me in my towel and carries me. She takes me past the big pool, and through the heavy door, and over the prickly floor.

She peels off my swimsuit and rubs me gently
with my towel. I see lots of kids with bare bottoms
and bare naked toes.

"Bare bottoms!" I laugh.

I wiggle away from Mama and run to the dryer that is on the wall. It shoots out warm air that blows my hair everywhere and takes away the wetness.

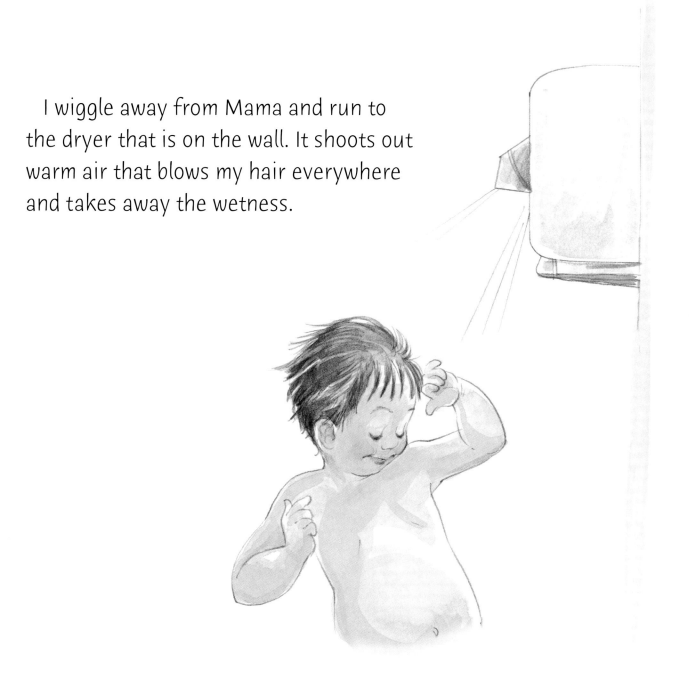

"Come on, John J.," she says.

I stand still. I like how the air feels on my hair. Mama brings my underwear, my pants, my shirt and my socks. I let her put them on me.

Mama carries me over the wet parts and
helps me with my boots. She kisses me.

I give Mama a hug. I snuggle on her shoulder
and she lifts me up. Mama's hair smells like
apples. She feels soft and cuddly and warm.

Mama sings my little song while we're walking through the doors.

"La la laaa. La la la laaa. La la laaa la la la laaa."

I close my eyes and fall asleep.

We acknowledge the support of the Canada Council for the Arts, the Ontario Arts Council, and the Government of Canada through the Book Publishing Industry Development Program (BPIDP) for our publishing activities.

Cataloguing in Publication Data

Farrell, Sue
        To the pool with mama

ISBN 1-55037-621-7 (bound) ISBN 1-55037-620-9 (pbk.)

I. Lewis, Robin Baird. II. Title.

PS8561.A78T6 2000   jC813'.54   C99-932360-1
PZ7.F37To 2000

The art in this book was rendered in watercolors.
The text was typeset in Humana Sans.

Distributed in Canada by:
Firefly Books Ltd.
3680 Victoria Park Avenue
Willowdale, ON
M2H 3K1

Published in the U.S.A. by Annick Press (U.S.) Ltd.
Distributed in the U.S.A. by:
Firefly Books (U.S.) Inc.
P.O. Box 1338
Ellicott Station
Buffalo, NY 14205

Printed and bound in Canada by
Friesens, Altona, Manitoba.

To the loves of my life: Tom, Shea & John J.
—S.F.

To Hunter & Neil, with thanks.
—R.B.L.